Larry Burkett's
Great Smoky Mountains Storybook Series

Sarah and the Art Contest

Written by
Larry Burkett
with **K. Christie Bowler**

Illustrated by **Terry Julien**

MOODY PRESS
CHICAGO

Dedicated to
Ryan Collins-Burkett

ℛm

Larry Burkett's Money Matters for Kids™
Executive Producer: *Allen Burkett*

For Lightwave
Managing Editor: *Elaine Osborne*
Art Director: *Terry Van Roon*
Desktop: *Andrew Jaster*

ISBN: 0-8024-0984-9

1 3 5 7 9 10 8 6 4 2

Printed in the United States of America

The Great Smoky Mountain Tales come to you from Larry Burkett's Money Matters for Kids™. In each tale, our family's children have fun while they learn how to best manage their money according to God's principles of stewardship.

This series of children's stories tells the adventures of the Carmichael family who live in a state park in the Great Smoky Mountains of North Carolina. The park is a beautiful setting, with a mist rising from the mountains like a smoky mist, giving them their name. Mom and Dad work in the park and, with their children Sarah, Joshua, and Carey, live in the rangers' compound not far inside the main park gate. Sarah, ten years old, is conscientious and loves doing things the right way. She has lots of energy, is artistic, and thinks before she acts. Her brother Joshua is eight and a half. Always doing something active, he's impulsive, adventurous, and eager to learn. Carey, their younger sister, is almost three and very cute. She loves doing whatever her sister and brother are doing. In the first four books of the series they learn how to save, how to give to the church, how to spend wisely, and how to earn money.

There's always something interesting going on in the Great Smoky Mountains, from hiking and horseback riding to fishing or panning for sapphires and rubies. Nearby, the town of Waynesville and, only a little farther away, the city of Asheville, provide all the family needs in the way of city amenities.

Through everyday adventures—from buying pet hamsters to dealing with the aftermath of a winter storm, from getting the right equipment in order to become an artist to going on summer camping trips—the children learn. Practical situations any child could face serve as the background for teaching about God's principles of stewardship.

Your children will love the stories and ask for more. Without even realizing it, they will, like our characters, learn in the middle of an adventure.

Sarah ran into the house waving a piece of paper excitedly. "Look what I found!" she called. "Can I enter it? Please? Can I?"

Her parents and grandparents were seated around the dining room table working on the huge puzzle Grandpa had just bought. "What is it?" Mom asked.

"An art contest." Sarah's smile filled her whole face. "I know I can do a good painting. Maybe I'll be an artist when I grow up!"

"When's the deadline?" Grandpa asked.

"Saturday morning by 10:00 o'clock. I only have five days."

"Hmm, that's not much time," Dad commented. "But I don't see why you can't enter."

"All right!" Sarah grinned. She spun in a circle, holding the contest entry to her chest.

Grandma laughed. "What kind of painting are you going to do?"

"Watercolor!" Sarah stated. She'd already thought about that. Suddenly she frowned. "Oh, no. I don't have any watercolors. I forgot. I used up all my old ones."

Joshua came to see what all the excitement was about. Sarah filled him in on her contest and the problem of no art supplies. Grandpa stroked his chin, deep in thought, then glanced at his wife and raised an eyebrow. She smiled and nodded. "Tell you what," he said, "we'll give you each $20 as a gift. That will help you get your art set, Sarah. And I know Joshua has been talking about a certain very special belt . . ."

"Wow!" Joshua said. "Thanks." He and Sarah gave their grandparents a big hug.

"You're welcome. Now make sure you get a good deal," Grandpa cautioned. "Check two or three different stores for the best price on the best product before you buy. You want good quality things, right?"

The kids nodded eagerly.

"You might even find one on sale. Like this puzzle," he added, nodding at the table. "I shopped around, then waited for a sale. I got it for 20 percent off."

"We'll shop carefully," the kids promised. "Thanks!"

The next day after school, the family drove into
Asheville. Sarah and Joshua had their money, ready to shop.
As soon as they arrived, they headed for the Hobby Shop and
straight to the watercolor section.

"Look at this!" Sarah said to Joshua. "It's beautiful!" She
held up a brightly packaged "Complete Art Kit." "It has
everything," she exclaimed. "Watercolors, felt pens, crayons,
pencils, erasers, paper . . . everything! And it's only $14.89."

"Sounds great," Joshua agreed. "But maybe you should
check out Puffy's Art Store first. Or call around to other

shops. I phoned around about my camper's survival belt. The one in Rough It sounds fantastic. I'm going to check it out today." He shrugged. "But if it's not, Camp-Out has a sale coming up. I'll wait for that."

"But I can't wait," Sarah said. "I only have four days to finish my picture and take it to the contest. Besides, this one looks perfect! And I'll have enough left over for us to get ice creams."

Joshua grinned. "Sounds great!"

When everyone had finished their shopping, they stopped for supper. "Did you get what you wanted?" Mom asked.

Sarah showed them her "Complete Art Kit" and told them all about it.

Joshua said, "The belt in Rough It wasn't that great. Camp-Out's belt is perfect but it's too expensive. I'm going to wait for their sale."

"Good idea," Dad agreed. "We'll make sure we go back for it."

By the time they got home it was bedtime. But Thursday after school Sarah headed straight for the kitchen table. She had promised Carey she could paint with her if she was careful.

"I be very careful," Carey agreed, nodding.

They opened the box and both oohed. "Look at all this stuff!" Sarah said.

"Lotsa crayons," Carey added.

The two girls got out paper, spread the art supplies out, and started on their projects. Sarah began a practice painting and Carey went to work with the crayons.

A few minutes later, the crayon Carey was working with broke.

Sarah frowned. "You're supposed to be careful, Carey," she said with a sigh.

"Was careful!" Carey stated. "It broke."

Sarah took a crayon and colored with it for a bit. Sure enough, it broke too. "Hmm. I guess they're not very strong or something. That's OK, Carey. Go ahead."

Sarah was having her own troubles. The blocks of paint were rock hard. She had to add a lot of water before she could get paint from them. Even then it was lumpy. She frowned and thought back to her old watercolors. They hadn't done this. She shrugged and kept working.

After a while some of the hairs in her brush started to come loose. They made funny lines and sloppy edges in her painting. She pulled the loose ones out and kept going.

Half an hour later Sarah paused and stepped back to see her painting from a distance. "Not too bad," she thought.

Carey's tongue stuck out as she worked. The crayons kept breaking into smaller and smaller pieces. Finally she stopped. "Too small," she said, holding out a piece of crayon.

Sarah sighed. "I guess they're not the best, huh? It's OK. It's not your fault."

Carey looked at the broken crayons, then decided her doll was probably lonely.

Sarah finished her practice picture and put her paints aside. Mom brought her a glass of juice. "Bedtime," she said. "Hey, that looks great. Nice and bright!"

Sarah smiled. "Wait 'til you see my contest painting!"

By Friday after school the colors in Sarah's practice painting had run together. Sarah frowned, then got right to work on her contest painting. She was getting used to the weird ways the paint went onto the paper. But the hairs coming out of her brush were getting frustrating. She tried other brushes in the set but the same thing happened.

Just before bedtime, Sarah finished her painting and proudly showed it to her family. It would dry overnight, and then Mom would take her to Waynesville to drop it off in the morning.

As soon as Sarah woke up on Saturday morning, she ran to see her painting.

"Oh, no!" she wailed. "What happened?" All the colors had run together until the whole thing was a muddy brown. And the paper had curled up until it was almost a circle. Her practice piece looked just as bad. Sarah wanted to cry.

Dad put his hand on her shoulder. "I'm sorry, Sarah," he said. "I guess those paints just aren't very good."

"Nor the crayons. Nor the brushes. Nor the paper. It's not supposed to curl up like that." Sarah looked sadly at her father. "I guess it wasn't such a good deal, after all, huh?" She looked back at her picture. "No way can I take this to the contest today. I guess you don't need to drive me in this morning, Mom," she added sadly.

"Can you make another one?"

"Not in time. And not with these paints! The kit looked so good. And it was cheap."

"It looked great last night," Joshua said, looking over her shoulder. "Too bad, Sarah."

That Friday after school, Dad drove Sarah and Joshua into Asheville. Sarah wanted to try taking her "Complete Art Kit" back. But a big sign in the store said, "ALL SALES FINAL!" She'd missed the contest and now she couldn't even do nice paintings for her family!

Camp-Out's sale was on, so Joshua got the better quality camper's survival belt for just $19.75. He wore it right away, pleased with how wisely he'd spent Grandpa's money.

Grandpa and Grandma were working on the puzzle when they got home. Joshua proudly showed them his belt.

Then Sarah told her sad story. "I guess my good deal wasn't really such a good deal," she concluded. "I should have listened to your advice, Grandpa. And yours, Josh."

"Sometimes when we're in a hurry, we get things that are cheaper up front," Grandpa agreed. "But they end up not being what we want or being more expensive because we have to replace them. I almost bought a smaller puzzle because I was impatient," he added. "But I'm glad I waited. Look!" The puzzle almost filled the table.

When they stopped for a snack before bed, Grandpa turned to Sarah. "How about if I help you shop around for a good art set?" he asked.

"That would be great!" Sarah said, eyes shining. "But—I don't have any money left."

"Well, we'll find out how much you'll need. I'm sure you can do odd jobs to earn it. How would that be?"

"Awesome!"

Saturday, while Joshua played with his belt and took it to show his friends, Sarah telephoned hobby shops and art supply stores. Grandpa checked the newspaper and the local Buy & Sell magazine. Then he called an artist friend of his.

"I know all about the 'Complete Art Kit,'" he laughed. "I bought one myself when I was a kid—and regretted it." He gave Grandpa the address and phone number of The Studio right in Waynesville where he buys his supplies. "They'll take good care of you."

When Sarah called them, she discovered they had a set they guaranteed for only $24.99.

The next time the family went to Waynesville, Sarah checked out the art set. It looked fantastic—way better than her other one! And it said "Quality Guaranteed" right on the box. Sarah asked in another store that sometimes carried art supplies. But they had nothing like the set in The Studio. So Sarah decided that was the set for her.

To help Sarah earn the money she needed for her art set, Mom and Dad gave her odd jobs. So did her grand-parents. Sarah washed the car, weeded the garden, ran

errands, and washed windows. She even did some jobs so well that she earned a bonus!

Then the long weekend came—the beginning of camping season. Sarah, Joshua, and Carey set up a lemonade stand near the firewood shed. They sold their juice for 25 cents a cup. The weekend was sunny and warm so the campground was busy and people were thirsty. The kids' juice was ice cold and delicious. They sold a lot and divided the money between the three of them. Sarah's share, after expenses, was $13.75.

Sarah finally had enough money for her art set! So, on a bright and fresh spring day, Dad drove her into Waynesville. They pulled up before The Studio, climbed out of the car, and went in. Sarah dashed right to the section with the art sets— and there it was: "Borough's Amateur Art Set (Quality Guaranteed)." The price on the tag had been marked down to $19.99!

"It's on sale!" Sarah exclaimed, eyes shining. "Now this is a good deal!"

Dad smiled and agreed. "Maybe you'll have enough to buy yourself some good quality watercolor paper."

"Hey, yeah!" Sarah ran to check out the paper.

The clerk asked Sarah if she needed any help.

"Yes, please. Can you tell me which is the best paper?" she asked.

The clerk told her about the different papers and why artists used them. She decided on semismooth paper that came in a block so it wouldn't curl. She had just enough money!

When they got home, Sarah opened her new art set. She couldn't help admiring it. It was much better than her first one. It didn't have as many different art materials, but she could tell each one was good quality. She cracked open her new pad of paper and planned her first painting.

Sarah made her picture bright and lively, like the spring day outside. She painted the cherry and apple trees in full bloom, covered with beautiful pink and white flowers. She checked the trees blossoming in their backyard to make sure her colors were right.

"That's beautiful!" Grandpa said, peeking over her shoulder. He and Grandma had dropped by to finish their puzzle. They were almost done. "You've got the trees just right."

"Thanks. This is for you Grandpa," Sarah explained. "It's a thank-you for your gift and for showing me how to spend my money wisely. Now I know how to get a good deal."

Grandpa took the picture home and put it on his dresser where he could look at it often.

A week later Dad lifted a new framed painting and hung it carefully on a nail on the kitchen wall. The rest of the family told him when it was straight. Then they all stood back to admire it.

Sarah sighed. "My first framed painting."

"It looks good there," Mom said.

"Pretty," Carey agreed.

"Hey, not bad," Joshua added. "Maybe you will be an artist!"

Dad cleared his throat and pulled something out of his pocket as if he were a magician. "Ahem. Miss Sarah, due to your outstanding artistic abilities, I have here an invitation to submit a painting of your choice to the Waynesville Junior Art Show in . . . three weeks."

Sarah squealed in excitement.

Dad laughed. "Part of the reason you bought that first art set was because you were in a hurry," he told her. "There's always another chance. Remember, you never have to sacrifice quality—even when you're in a hurry."

Be a Wise Spender!

"She considers a field and buys it. She uses some of the money she earns to plant a vineyard" (Proverbs 31:16 NIrV).

Spending is not the opposite of saving, it's the opposite of earning. Saving is simply delayed spending. Even giving is spending your money on others. The key to spending is to be a wise steward of how you spend your money and what you spend it on. You'll spend all of your money eventually, anyway, so it's important to know how to spend it well.

Spending Well

Before you go out and spend that money that's burning a hole in your pocket, you need to take care of first things first. Your top priority when you spend your money should be to pay your bills and take care of needs, like library fines and club or lesson fees. After they're paid, then you can spend your spending money on things you want.

All right, you're ready. You might think spending's a snap. True, all you have to do is walk into a store, pick something up, and pay for it at the cashier. But is that thing really what you want? How do you know you're getting something you'll be happy with? Will it break right away? Slow down and take it one step at a time. If you want to be an ace at spending, there are four general rules you'll need to learn and follow.

1. You don't have to buy anything. And you don't have to have it now.
2. When you do spend, do it wisely by spending on things God approves of and by making sure you get good value for your money.
3. Don't spend it all right away. Plan to spend a certain amount, then stick to that plan.
4. Only spend the money you have, not the money you think you'll get.

Shop 'Til You Drop
but Don't Spend 'Til the End

How do you make sure you're getting good quality for your money? Here are some tips; follow them and you won't regret it: Never spend over a certain amount, say ten dollars, on impulse. Take the time to compare prices. Call different stores to see what they have and what sales are coming up. Look for used items for sale in the newspaper or your local Buy & Sell paper. Look into warranties: how long are they for and what do they cover? Check and see if you can return the item if it doesn't work properly.

Most of your shopping will be done before you even think of actually spending and often before you have the money saved. By the time you're ready, you'll know what you want, what kind of price you're looking at, and where the best deals are. Spend only at the very end of your shopping.

When you do the work, shop around, and finally buy something of good quality that you really like, you'll want to do it again. And all that money you save? Buy something else you've been wanting. Wise spending pays off. Guaranteed!

Larry Burkett's **Money Matters for Kids**™ provides practical tips and tools children need to understand the biblical principles of stewardship. **Money Matters for Kids**™ is committed to the next generation and is grounded in God's Word and living His principles. Its goal is *"Teaching Kids to Manage God's Gifts."*

Money Matters for Kids™ and **Money Matters for Teens**™ materials are adapted by **Lightwave Publishing**™ from the works of best selling author on business and personal finances, **Larry Burkett.** Larry is the founder and president of **Christian Financial Concepts**™, author of more than 50 books, and hosts a radio program "Money Matters" aired on more than 1,100 outlets worldwide. Money Matters for Kids™ has an entertaining and educational Web site for children, teens, and college students, along with a special **Financial Parenting**™ Resource section for adults.

Visit Money Matters for Kids Web site at: **www.mm4kids.org**

building Christian faith in families

Lightwave Publishing is a recognized leader in developing quality resources that encourage, assist, and equip parents to build Christian faith in their families.

Lightwave Publishing also has a fun kids' Web site and an internet-based newsletter called *Tips & Tools for Spiritual Parenting*. This newsletter helps parents with issues such as answering their children's questions, helping make church more exciting, teaching children how to pray, and much more.

For more information, visit Lightwave's Web site: **www.lightwavepublishing.com**

MOODY
The Name You Can Trust
A MINISTRY OF MOODY BIBLE INSTITUTE

Moody Press, a ministry of Moody Bible Institute, is designed for education, evangelization, and edification.

If we may assist you in knowing more about Christ and the Christian life, please write us without obligation:

Moody Press, c/o MLM Chicago, Illinois 60610.

Or visit us at Moody's Web site: **www.moodypress.org**